Silver Secrets

First published August 1991.

ISBN: 0-89486-777-6

Printed in the United States of America.

Library of Congress Catalog Card Number: 91-72471

Editor's note:
   Hazelden Educational Materials offers a variety of
information on chemical dependency and related areas.
Our publications do not necessarily represent Hazelden's
programs, nor do they officially speak for any Twelve Step
organization.

About the author:
   Stephen Roos was born in New York City and grew up
in Connecticut. He graduated from Yale and worked in
publishing before becoming a professional writer. In addi-
tion to the Maple Street Kids stories, he is the author of the
New Eden Kids series and the Pet Lovers Club books.
Stephen Roos makes his home in New York State's Hudson
River Valley.

Silver Secrets

Stephen Roos

Illustrated by Steve Premo

Chapter One

It was Independence Day.

American flags flew from the houses.

The high school band marched down Maple Street. It was playing "Stars and Stripes Forever" as loudly as it could.

Then came the men and women who had been in the army, navy, marines, and the air force.

Behind the band were the Cub Scouts and the Brownies.

Then came the Girl Scouts and Boy Scouts.

The crowd on the sidewalk waved little flags and cheered.

Augie and Darryl stood at the front of the crowd.

They were cheering too.

In the fall, they were joining the Cubs.

Next year they'd be in the parade too.

Augie was the kid with the blond crew cut.

Darryl was the kid with all the curly black hair and the eyebrows that met above his nose.

They were carrying aluminum trays covered with silver foil.

Under Augie's silver foil were slices of juicy, pink watermelon.

Under Darryl's silver foil were three dozen of his mother's triple-triple chocolate fudge brownies.

Like everyone else, they were on their way to the Fourth of July picnic in the park.

The sun was beginning to dip behind the bandshell now.

It would be dark soon.

Then there would be fireworks.

As far as Augie was concerned, fireworks were better than parades.

They were even better than brownies, and Darryl's mom's brownies were as good as brownies could get. Augie pushed his tongue against the tooth at the front of his mouth.

It was Augie's last baby tooth.

"It's driving me crazy, Darryl," he groaned.

"My dad ties one end of a string to your tooth and the other end of it to the doorknob," Darryl explained. "Then he slams the door."

"Does it hurt?"

"Oh, something awful," Darryl said. "But it works, Augie. You want a brownie?"

Darryl pushed some of the silver foil aside and held the tray out to Augie.

"What I want is a painless tooth extractor!" Augie sighed.

"Why don't you invent one?" Darryl asked. "You're going to be an inventor when you grow up, aren't you?"

"I'm already an inventor," Augie reminded Darryl.

He jammed his tongue against the tooth again.

Nothing. The tooth still wouldn't come out.

"It would make a million, wouldn't it?"

"What would make a million?" Darryl asked.

"Augie Wade's Super Painless Tooth Extractor!" Augie said happily. If he hadn't been afraid of dropping the watermelon slices, he would have jumped up and down. "Everyone's going to go for it! Tomorrow you can help me scout for parts."

"Maybe," Darryl sighed.

"But it could be my greatest invention ever!" Augie exclaimed.

"You ever think I might have something else to do?" Darryl asked.

"Like what?"

"I don't have to tell you *everything*," Darryl said.

Augie felt hurt. "I tell *you* everything," he said. "Best friends always tell each other everything, Darryl."

"Whatever you want to do, you always expect me to do it too. You don't even ask me. You kind of just tell me, Augie."

"Do not," Augie insisted.

"Do too," Darryl said.

"Well, you're younger than I am," Augie reminded him.

"By two months is all!" Darryl said. "And I'm just as tall."

"Because you got big hair," Augie said. "If you had a crew cut, you'd be two inches shorter."

"Well, you shouldn't treat me like a little kid," Darryl said.

"You shouldn't keep secrets from me," Augie said.

The boys walked to the corner.

Not saying a word.

They waited for the policeman to let them cross the street.

More and more people were gathering at the entrance of the park.

Men were selling balloons.

And tiny little flags.

And cotton candy.

"You mad at me?" Darryl asked.

"You mad at *me?*" Augie said.

"Take a brownie," Darryl said.

He held out the tray.

Augie lifted the silver foil.

He took a brownie.

"Don't throw the silver foil away," Darryl said.

"What is it with you and silver foil, anyway?" Augie asked. "Why are you always saving it?"

"I like anything silver," Darryl said. "It's my favorite color."

"But what do you do with it?" Augie asked.

"None of your bee's wax," Darryl said. He grabbed the foil from Augie and stuffed it in his pocket.

Augie bit off a piece of the brownie.

6

He started to chew.

He chewed some more.

"You like it?" Darryl asked.

"It's delicious," Augie admitted. "But I'm still not talking to you, Darryl. Until you stop keeping secrets from me."

"That's okay," Darryl said. "I'll probably never talk to you again."

The light changed.

The boys crossed the street.

Augie saw his mom spreading the blankets on the lawn.

Darryl's dad was standing at the barbecue.

Darryl's mom was opening a wicker picnic basket.

Augie pushed his tongue against the loose tooth again.

"It's gone!" Augie said.

"What's gone?" Darryl asked.

"My tooth!" Augie cried. "Oh, gosh! I must have swallowed it!"

"You didn't swallow it!" Darryl said.

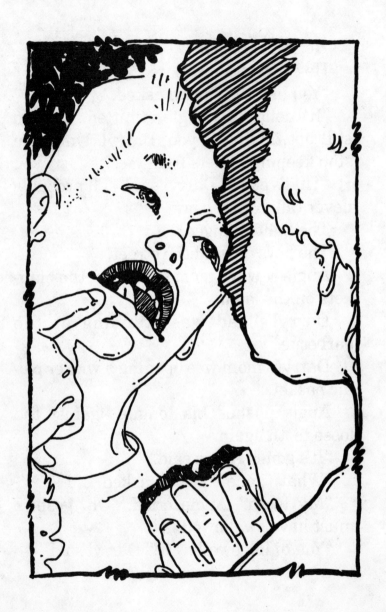

Darryl pointed to the rest of the brownie in Augie's hand.

Augie's tooth was stuck where he'd bitten into it.

"Didn't you feel anything?" Darryl asked.

Augie shook his head.

"I guess my mom's a better inventor than you are, Augie!" Darryl giggled.

"Your mom's no inventor!" Augie insisted.

Darryl was laughing out loud now. "She invented the Super Painless Tooth Extractor before you did!"

Augie made a face.

He wanted to stay mad at Darryl for a little while longer.

But he couldn't help himself.

In a moment he was laughing too.

That was the trouble with having a best friend like Darryl.

No matter how hard Augie tried, he just couldn't stay mad at Darryl very long.

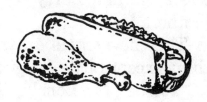

Chapter Two

Even if there were times Augie didn't like Darryl Lenski too much, he *always* liked Darryl's mom and dad.

They were always nice.

Ever since Augie's dad had died, they had included Augie and his mom in just about everything.

Mr. Lenski was very, very thin.

Mrs. Lenski was very fat.

Sometimes some of the kids made fun of her.

Augie never did.

Darryl's dad was barbecuing some chicken and some hot dogs.

"Hope you boys worked up an appetite," he said. "When Harold and Barry come back from Little League, we'll all eat."

Harold and Barry were Darryl's older brothers.

They never paid any attention to anything except Little League.

"You bet, Mr. Lenski," Augie said.

Augie gave his mom the tray of watermelon.

Darryl put the tray of fudge brownies on the picnic table.

Mrs. Lenski was putting a platter of barbecued chicken in the middle of the blanket.

She reached for a leg and took a bite from it.

"You want some, Augie?"

Augie took a wing. It was delicious.

Mrs. Lenski was wiping some sweat off her forehead.

"You feeling okay, Doris?" Augie's mom asked.

"I'm just fine," Mrs. Lenski said. "It's my nerves. I just need one of my little pills. Darryl, get me some lemonade, will you, honey? So I can swallow my pill?"

Augie watched Darryl open the thermos. He saw the look on Darryl's face. Even if Darryl never said anything about it, Augie knew Darryl was worried about his mom.

The year before, she had become dizzy in the supermarket and fainted. The store manager had called the rescue squad and an ambulance had taken her to the hospital.

They had given her pills. They were supposed to keep her calm. But Mrs. Lenski was more nervous than ever lately. It seemed she was always opening up one of her little pill bottles and taking another pill.

Darryl handed his mom the cup.

Mrs. Lenski took three of the little pills and swallowed them down with the lemonade.

Three pills. Not one, like she said.

Augie wondered if Darryl had noticed too.

"Cotton candy! Get your cotton candy! Only fifty cents!" a man by the fountain was shouting.

"Mom?" Augie asked.

His mother was already pulling a dollar bill from her wallet. "For Darryl too," she said. "My treat."

"Thanks Mrs. Wade," Darryl said.

The boys ran over to the cotton candy stand.

Right in front of them were Rooney and Tara.

They were going to be fourth graders next fall too.

As far as Augie could figure, Rooney had never learned to talk. She shouted everything. She was always getting into trouble too.

Tara was the quietest girl in school. She never got into trouble.

How Rooney and Tara got to be best friends, Augie would never understand.

14

"We're going over to the fireworks now!" Rooney shouted. She gave the man two quarters and he gave her the cotton candy. It was pink and almost as big as her head.

"But it won't be dark for another twenty minutes," Augie said.

"If we don't get there early, we won't get the good seats," Tara explained.

"We want to be right *under* the fireworks!" Rooney shouted. "That's how it's best!"

That was what Augie wanted!

He ran back to the grown-ups.

"Can we go to the fireworks now, Ma?" he asked. "Darryl too, Mrs. Lenski?"

"But we have all this wonderful food, boys," Mr. Lenski said.

"Bring the food," Darryl said. "We don't want to miss the best seats!"

"I don't think I can," Mrs. Lenski said. "I don't feel up to moving now."

Augie could see she was looking very pale. She was sweating more too, even though it wasn't hot today.

"Maybe we should take you home, Doris," Mr. Lenski suggested.

"I'll be fine," she said. "Maybe just another one of those pills."

"You boys run along," Mrs. Wade said. "We'll save some food for you guys for later."

The boys ran back to Tara and Rooney.

They all had their cotton candy now.

Augie bit into his.

"It's weird," he said.

"Bad weird?" Tara asked.

"All tingly and a little scratchy," Augie said. "And it disappears the minute you taste it."

"You mean funny weird," Tara said. "Not bad weird."

"That's it," Augie said. "Funny weird."

The kids walked to the top of the hill.

On the other side was the lake.

The kids raced down the hill.

They kicked off their shoes and stuck their feet in the water.

Except for Rooney.

She was teetering on the edge of the water.

16

As though she were on the tight rope at the circus.

"I'm going to fall! I'm going to fall!" she shouted.

"Don't you dare!" Tara shouted back at her.

But it was too late.

Splash!

Dunk!

Splash!

Rooney was in the lake.

The water came all the way up to her waist.

"You did that on purpose," Tara said to her.

"Did not!" Rooney shouted.

"Did too!" Tara said as she pulled Rooney out.

She was sopping wet.

But that never bothered Rooney.

It was getting dark. The lights in the Japanese lanterns glowed.

The workers on the other side of the lake were getting the fireworks ready.

More and more people gathered on the grass behind the kids.

"Waiting's the worst thing ever," Tara said.

"It'll be worth it," Rooney said. "Don't you worry."

Augie was getting excited.

"How're you doing, Darryl?" he asked. "You getting excited?"

Darryl shrugged. "I guess so," he said. "I wish the grown-ups were here."

"It's better without grown-ups," Rooney said. "Everything is better without grown-ups, I think."

18

But Augie knew that Darryl meant his mother.

From the way Darryl was biting his lower lip, Augie could see Darryl was worried.

There was a roar in the distance.

"It's the fireworks," Rooney cried. "They're about to start!"

"Not yet," Tara said. "It's not dark enough!"

The noise was louder now. It was coming nearer.

"It's a siren!" Rooney shouted.

"Fire engines?" Augie asked. "You think something's on fire?"

Darryl was standing up. "It's an ambulance," he said anxiously.

"How can you tell?" Augie asked.

"I remember from when my mom was in the supermarket," Darryl said. "It's just like that!"

Darryl started to run up the hill. He was darting through the crowd.

Augie ran after him. "Stay here, Darryl!" he yelled. "You don't want to miss the fireworks!"

"I can't," Darryl cried. "Something's wrong with my mom. I know it is!"

He ran faster.

Augie ran after him. "You worry too much, Darryl!" Augie yelled.

20

But Darryl ran faster and faster. It was the first time Darryl had ever outrun Augie.

The boys ran all the way back to the picnic grounds.

When they got there, there was a crowd gathered where Mrs. Wade and the Lenskis had been sitting.

Darryl pushed his way through the people.

Augie pushed too.

At the center of the crowd was the ambulance.

Mrs. Lenski was lying on a stretcher and two men were putting her into the back of the ambulance.

Chapter Three

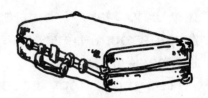

Orange juice.

Corn Flakes.

A slice of toast with grape jelly.

There wasn't anything special about breakfast this morning.

No cotton candy. No fudge brownies.

July Fourth was over.

Augie took another spoonful of his cereal. The comics were laid in front of him, but he wasn't looking at them. He was looking at his mom instead.

She was on the phone with Mr. Lenski, but mostly she was listening. When she did say something, it was very quiet and only a couple of words.

They were talking about Mrs. Lenski.

The night before, at the July Fourth picnic, Mr. Lenski had gone with her in the ambulance. Augie's mom had followed in her car. Darryl had sat up front with Augie's mom. Barry and Harold had sat in the back with Augie.

His mom kept saying everything was going to be okay, but Augie had been scared. Scared for Darryl. Scared for Barry and Harold too, even if they *were* a lot older. Scared something was really wrong again with Mrs. Lenski.

When they got to the hospital, Mrs. Lenski was in the emergency room. Mr. Lenski was still with her.

Mrs. Wade and the boys waited outside.

It had taken almost an hour till the doctor had said Mrs. Lenski was out of danger.

"When will she be well enough to leave the hospital?" Augie's mother had asked.

"Not too long," the doctor had said. "But she's going to have to go to a rehabilitation center afterwards."

"What's that?" Harold had asked.

"It's where your mom can learn to deal with her addiction," the doctor had said.

Addiction.

The word made Augie uncomfortable.

He remembered the two men at school assembly last year.

One said he used to be an alcoholic. He drank beer and wine all the time. Finally, he got so sick he lost his job and his home and ended up living on the streets.

The other man had used drugs. He spent a year in jail for selling them too.

Both men said they were addicts.

Augie thought about Mrs. Lenski. He couldn't see how she was like that.

She had never been in jail.

She had never lived on the streets.

Augie tried not to think about it.

At the hospital, the doctor said no one except Mr. Lenski could see her till the next day. Not even Darryl or Barry or Harold.

Mrs. Wade had driven everyone home. No one said a word the whole time. Augie wondered if they were thinking what he was thinking.

Mrs. Lenski was an addict?

It wasn't so. It *couldn't* be!

The memory of the night before faded as Augie took a bite of his toast.

He watched his mom hang up the phone.

"Mr. Lenski says they're going to hire a housekeeper," Mrs. Wade said. "Until then the boys are going to stay with their aunt out of town."

"When are they going?"

"This morning," Mrs. Wade said.

Augie went to the window. The Lenski boys were bringing suitcases out of their house. They were putting them into their car.

"I got to say good-bye," Augie said.

"Me too," Mrs. Wade said.

They ran down the back steps and across the lawn to the Lenskis'.

"I'm going to miss you, Darryl," Augie said.

"It won't be too long," Darryl said.

"You shouldn't feel bad," Augie said. "I mean, your mom is going to be getting better, isn't she?"

"She'll be okay," Darryl said. "I know it'll be okay."

But Augie could tell Darryl wasn't feeling so sure about it. He patted Darryl on the shoulder.

Mr. Lenski got in the car and started the motor.

"Hey, wait a minute," Augie said. "Nobody leave yet!"

He ran back into his house.

He raced up the stairs.

He went to the dresser in the corner of his room.

On top of it was a silver dollar. The one Uncle Bret had given him last year on his eighth birthday.

That made it special to Augie. It would be special to Darryl because it was silver. And because it was from Augie.

He grabbed it and ran down the stairs.

Through the kitchen.

Across the yard.

To the Lenskis' car.

Darryl was sitting by the window.

"Here, Darryl, you take it," Augie said.

"It's your special silver dollar," Darryl said.

"You take it," Augie said. "For when you feel bad. Maybe it'll make you feel a little better."

"But it's just a loan," Darryl said. "I'll give it to you when I come back."

"It's a deal," Augie said.

Mr. Lenski put the car into reverse.

He backed the car onto the street.

Augie and his mom stood on the sidewalk, waving.

The Lenskis waved back.

A moment later, the car turned the corner and was out of sight.

Chapter Four

It was three days since Darryl had gone to his aunt's.

Augie's mom said Augie should play with some of the other kids, but he didn't feel like it.

Augie sat on the edge of his bed and looked around his room.

His mom said it was the worst mess in the world.

But it wasn't a mess. It was Augie's laboratory.

A plastic toilet paper roller on the window sill.

The training wheels from his first bike on his dresser.

Two pipes the plumber had left behind leaning against the closet door.

Knobs from every appliance that had ever been thrown out on Maple Street.

Plus one hundred other odds and ends he had collected from all over the place.

Somewhere in that stuff were all the parts he needed to make the painless tooth extractor. Only Augie couldn't see it.

He went downstairs.

His mother was watching her soap opera.

"I'm going out, Ma," he said.

"To play with the kids?" his mother asked.

"Nah," Augie said. "I want to get some stuff for my inventions."

He walked outside. He passed the Lenskis' house. It was still empty. The lawn had missed a mowing.

He walked down Maple Street. When the light changed, he walked through the park.

Mrs. Ames's house was on the other side, almost a block farther. Workmen were still hammering and sawing away at her garage. They were putting a big skylight in the roof now. When they were through, Mrs. Ames's garage was going to be an artist's studio.

The scrap pile in her driveway was still getting bigger.

Augie saw a pulley stuck under a board. He stepped closer.

"Scavenging again, Augie?"

It was Mrs. Ames. Even though she had retired last spring from teaching art at their elementary school, she wasn't all that old-looking. Her hair wasn't even gray yet. It was black and she wore it in a ponytail. In the summer she wore a big straw hat because her skin was sensitive.

"It's okay, isn't it?" Augie asked cautiously.

"If it can help a struggling young inventor, I'm all for it," Mrs. Ames said.

Augie raised the board and set it aside. He reached for the pulley. The rope was still in it.

"What's it going to be?" Mrs. Ames asked.

Augie let his tongue play with the hole where his tooth had been. "A painless tooth extractor," he said. "For Darryl when he comes home."

"But Darryl's lost all his baby teeth," Mrs. Ames said.

Augie hadn't thought about that.

"Well, I was saving the automatic bed-maker till Christmas," he said.

"That sounds wonderful," Mrs. Ames said. "Make it now, Augie."

Augie wanted to ask Mrs. Ames something. It was something he'd been afraid to ask anyone else. But Mrs. Ames had been at the school assembly, the one with the two men who had been addicts.

"The doctor said Mrs. Lenski's an addict," Augie said. "It's not true, is it?"

"Why couldn't it be true?" Mrs. Ames said.

"But she can't be like that," Augie insisted. "Mrs. Lenski is nice. She takes a lot of pills, but the doctor gave them to her.

34

They're for her nerves, some of them. Some of them are for her weight. She's not anything like the men at the assembly last spring."

Mrs. Ames put her hand on Augie's shoulder.

She sat down beside the maple tree.

Augie sat down too.

"The pills *are* drugs, Augie," she said. "It doesn't matter who gives them to you."

"But it's not like marijuana or cocaine or anything like that," Augie said. "They're legal."

"But they're still drugs," Mrs. Ames said.

"Why didn't she stop using them?" Augie asked. "Couldn't she have tried harder?"

"It's not about trying hard enough," Mrs. Ames said. "When someone is addicted, no matter how hard they try, they can't seem to stop using alcohol or other drugs."

"How come?" Augie asked.

"No one knows for sure," Mrs. Ames said. "But it doesn't have anything to do with being nice or not nice."

"But they're punishing her for it," Augie explained. "That's why she's going to have to spend the rest of the summer in some funny place, like that drug addict who went to jail."

"The rehabilitation center?" Mrs. Ames asked.

Augie nodded.

"It's not punishment, Augie," Mrs. Ames said. "It's not a prison at all. It's like a hospital. She's with people who can show her she doesn't need the pills. When she comes home, she'll be meeting more people with her problem. They'll help each other, so they can all get better."

"You sure?" Augie asked.

"It's what happened in my family."

"You have a relative who takes pills too much?" Augie asked.

"Well, it was different from pills," Mrs. Ames said. "But it was addiction. It took time, Augie. It'll take a lot of work on Mrs. Lenski's part," Mrs. Ames added. "And she'll

need her family to be real under-
standing too. And the family is going to
need their friends to help too."

"But what am I supposed to do, Mrs.
Ames?" Augie asked. "I'm just a kid."

"Making Darryl an automatic bed-maker
sounds like just the thing, Augie," Mrs.
Ames said. "Let him know how much he
means to you."

Augie sighed.

He didn't see how an invention, even the
Fabulous Automatic Bed-Maker, was going
to help.

But he knew that wasn't going to keep
him from trying.

Chapter Five

Ding
Dong.

Augie opened the front door.

It was Tara. She was holding a batch of envelopes in her hand.

"It's for my party," she said as she handed him an envelope with his name on the front. "I sure hope you can come, Augie."

Augie opened the envelope.

Teddy bears.

Yuck.

But Tara was so nice that Augie couldn't hold the teddy bears against her.

"It's tomorrow, three o'clock," Tara said, smiling. "Oh, and don't forget to bring your bathing suit. We got a pool this year."

"You going to have another food fight?" Augie asked.

"Oh, gosh," Tara sighed. "I hope not!"

Augie remembered last year.

Ice cream and chocolate cake all over everything, including Tara's cocker spaniel.

Everyone said it had been the best birthday party ever.

Except Tara.

It had taken her a whole day to clean up her dog.

"There's no one home at the Lenskis'," Tara said. She took another envelope. "Could you please give this one to Darryl when you see him?" Tara asked.

Augie heard a car door slam.

The Lenskis' car was in their driveway. Augie saw Harold and Barry and Darryl getting out.

"Darryl's home!" Augie shouted. He raced upstairs. There, in the middle of his room, was the automatic bed-maker.

It had taken him almost four days to put the pulley and the rope and aluminum poles and the clothespins together.

But it had been worth it. The automatic bed-maker was his best invention ever. Augie couldn't wait to give it to Darryl. He knew how much Darryl was going to love it.

Augie grabbed the pulley and the rope and the poles. It was almost too much for him to carry.

"Come on, Tara," he said when he got to the front porch. "You can give Darryl the invitation yourself!"

Augie raced down the front steps and across the lawn.

Tara was only a foot or two behind.

"Darryl! Darryl!" Augie shouted. "Look what I got you!"

Darryl was carrying his little blue suit-case.

"What you got there?" he asked.

"It's for you, Darryl," he said. "Kind of a welcome back gift."

"Welcome home, Darryl," Tara said. "I hope you'll come to my birthday party. It's tomorrow afternoon."

She handed him his invitation.

"I don't know if I can," Darryl said hesitantly.

"Oh, you've got to," Augie said. "All the guys are going to be there."

"Well, not *all* the *guys*," Tara said. "You two are the only guys."

"How come?" Augie asked.

"On account of Marcus being in PeeWee League and Norris being at the shore and Lem being at camp," Tara said. "But all the girls are coming," she added happily.

"You got to come," Augie said to Darryl. "You're not going to let me be the only boy there, are you?"

"I'll check it out with my dad first," Darryl said.

Harold and Barry were following their father into the house with the rest of the luggage.

Augie laid the invention out on the grass.

43

Tara and Darryl stood closer.

"Well, it's very pretty," Tara said pleasantly. "I can't tell just what it is exactly."

"You take a look, Darryl," Augie said. "I bet you can figure it out."

Darryl picked up the pulley. He moved the rope through it. He pointed one of the poles at Augie.

"Is it some kind of torture instrument?" he asked.

"It's an automatic bed-maker!" Augie exclaimed. "It's what you always wanted. You know how your mom is always telling you to make your bed."

Darryl frowned.

Augie wondered if he shouldn't talk about Mrs. Lenski anymore. Not until she was back home too.

Darryl looked again.

He looked closer.

He looked harder.

"I still don't see it, Augie," he sighed.

"I'll show you how it works!" Augie said.

He knelt beside it.

"You screw the pulley to the ceiling over your bed. All you do is wrap your bedspread around the poles. You connect the pillow to the clothespins and then you pull the rope when you get out of bed. That's all there is to it!"

"Gosh, I bet that'll save a lot of time," Tara said.

"Let's install it now," Augie said. "We'll time it."

"We're supposed to meet Miss Berns now," Darryl said.

"Who's she?" Tara asked.

"The housekeeper Dad hired," Darryl said.

"I can come over later," Augie said.

"I don't know about later," Darryl said.

"Aren't you feeling okay?" Augie asked.

"It's a long trip from my aunt's," Darryl said.

"So you're tired. You need to rest," Tara said. "Tomorrow you'll feel better. You'll come to my party and it'll be like always."

"I've got to go inside, Augie," Darryl said. "Thanks for the invitation, Tara."

"Oh, sure," Tara said. Augie and Tara watched Darryl go inside his house.

"He didn't seem to think much of my invention," Augie said. "I don't think he was very happy to see *me* either."

"He's tired," Tara said. "That's all."

"He's different," Augie said.

Augie and Tara walked across the grass.

"Well, his mother's sick," Tara said.

"But *he's* not sick," Augie said. "I think he's acting weird, Tara."

"You mean funny weird?" Tara asked. "Like the cotton candy?"

Augie shook his head.

He meant *bad* weird.

46

Chapter Six

The present looked nice enough.

Blue paper.

Green ribbons.

But it wasn't anything Augie would give anyone. Even a girl.

It was hair ribbons. His mom had bought them. Yuck. But his mom said that's what girls liked.

Most of the other kids were already there. Standing at one end of the swimming pool.

All girls. Another yuck.

Beth.

And Felicity.

And Lisa.

And Kimberly.

And Rooney.

And Tara, of course.

Most of them were in their bathing suits. Except Tara who was wearing a dress. And Rooney who was wearing blue jeans as usual.

"Darryl didn't come with you?" Tara asked.

"I saw him this morning," Augie said. "He said he'd meet me here."

Augie checked his wristwatch. Quarter after three. Darryl wasn't the kind to be late. For birthday cakes and ice cream especially.

"You guys want to play softball?" Augie asked. "I could go home and get my bat."

"I already brought my bat," Rooney said.

"But I don't like baseball," Beth said.

"I can't play softball in my new dress," Tara said.

"Well, what are we supposed to play?" Augie asked.

"I like playing dolls," Felicity said.

"Dolls?" Augie asked. "I can't play dolls!"

48

"We're too old for dolls now," Tara reminded Felicity.

"We are?" Felicity asked.

"No one plays dolls after age seven," Tara pointed out.

"No one?" Felicity asked sadly.

"I was always too old for dolls," Rooney said.

"No dolls then," Tara said.

"We could play volleyball," Rooney said.

"In the pool!" Augie suggested. He liked water volleyball.

"Girls against the boys!" Lisa said.

"You mean girls against the boy, don't you?" Rooney laughed.

"I don't have a net," Tara said. "My dog ate it."

"I guess no water volleyball," Augie said. He looked at his wristwatch again. Where was Darryl? It was getting later and later. Augie couldn't decide whether he should be worried or mad.

"Well, there's always house," Beth said. "That's my favorite."

"Oh, house!" Felicity and Lisa said excitedly.

"House?" Augie asked uncertainly. "I never heard of house."

"You can be the daddy," Kimberly said.

"And Tara can be the mommy!" Felicity said.

"And we'll be the kids," Beth said.

"Except I'm not going to be some kid," Rooney said. "I'll be the hold-up guy."

"There's no hold-up guys in house," Tara said.

"You can be the rotten kid," Beth said.

"And when the daddy comes home from the office, everyone kisses him," Lisa said.

"No way!" Rooney said.

"Okay," Beth said, "everyone except Rooney kisses the daddy."

"That's how we know you're rotten, Rooney," Tara said sweetly.

"You kiss the daddy?" Augie asked.

It wasn't the first time Augie had ever felt scared.

But it was the first time he had ever been frightened at someone's birthday party.

50

If Darryl were here, none of this would be happening.

He wasn't going to be worried about Darryl any longer.

From now on, he was just going to be mad.

"Okay," Lisa said. "It's five o'clock and the daddy's just coming home from a hard day at the office and we all kiss him."

"Oh, don't bother," Augie assured her. "We can just sit down to dinner right away."

"But we always kiss the daddy when he comes home from the office," Beth insisted.

"But it wasn't a hard day at the office," Augie said.

"It was a *horrible* day," Lisa said.

"The big deal just fell through," Beth said.

"And your boss fired you," Kimberly added.

"And you need us all to kiss you a lot," Felicity said.

The girls were stepping toward him.

Their arms were stretched out toward him.

Kimberly had her eyes closed.

Felicity was doing funny things with her lips.

It was the most frightening thing Augie had ever seen.

He panicked.

He took three steps back.

Never in his life had he so much wanted to run away.

Suddenly he saw Tara's mom on the patio. She was holding the cake. All the candles were lit. Eight of them, plus one to grow on.

It was like a miracle.

"Happy birthday to you!" Augie sang out as loud as he could.

"Happy birthday to you," Tara's mother sang.

All at once the girls turned around.

"Happy birthday dear Tara," the girls sang along.

"Happy birthday to you," everybody was singing now.

All the girls gathered around Tara.

She took a deep breath.

She blew out all the candles.

All the girls cheered.

But Augie hardly heard them.

He was already on his way out of there.

As fast as his legs could carry him.

Past the swimming pool.

Around the side of Tara's house.

Back to the street.

On his way home.

It had been horrible.

Five girls almost kissed him!

He had just barely escaped from the worst experience of his life!

And it was all Darryl's fault.

Chapter Seven

"He didn't show, Mom!" Augie moaned as loud as he could moan.

He let the kitchen door slam behind him.

"I was the only boy at Tara's birthday party," he said. "It was the most horrible experience of my life."

"Well, I bet you liked the ice cream and cake," his mother said.

"It was so awful I couldn't stay for dessert," Augie said. "They wanted to play house, Mom! They almost kissed me!"

"Oh, Augie," his mother sighed. "I'd no idea how dangerous a birthday party could be."

"It's not funny, Mom! And it's all Darryl's fault too. He shouldn't have let me down like that!"

"Honey, I'm sure Darryl had a very good reason," Mrs. Wade said.

"He should have told me the reason, Mom!" Augie said.

"Maybe he couldn't, Augie."

Augie looked through the kitchen window.

Outside he could see Darryl's house.

He saw the back door open.

He saw Darryl step outside.

"There he is now," his mom said. "Why don't you talk to him about it?"

"He should talk to me first," Augie insisted.

"Augie!" his mother said sharply.

Augie stood up.

He shrugged and went out the back door.

"Hey, there, Darryl," he called.

Darryl didn't look up.

He was cramming a bag into the garbage can.

56

"What happened?" Augie asked.

Darryl jumped.

He tried to slam the lid on the garbage can.

"Sorry, Augie," Darryl said. "I guess I didn't hear you."

"Darryl," Augie said firmly. "I want to know why you didn't come to Tara's party."

"Was it this afternoon?" Darryl asked.

"You know it was this afternoon," Augie said. "We talked about it this morning."

"I guess I forgot since this morning," Darryl said.

He was fussing with the top of the garbage can, trying to press it down on the garbage.

"I was the only boy," Augie said. "It was awful."

"Sorry," Darryl said.

But he seemed to be more concerned with the garbage can lid than with Augie.

"I was the only boy there, Darryl! Me and six girls. And except for Rooney, they all wanted to kiss me. It was awful, Darryl."

"I said I was sorry," Darryl said.

"Sorry doesn't make me feel better," Augie explained.

Darryl pushed harder on the garbage can lid.

But he couldn't push hard enough.

The lid wasn't staying on.

"You got too much in the can," Augie said. "Let me do it."

"I can do it myself!" Darryl exclaimed loudly.

"No, you can't," Augie said.

He pulled the lid from Darryl's hands.

He dropped it on the ground.

"Leave the garbage alone!" Darryl said.

"But you got too much in the can," Augie said.

Augie reached for the bag Darryl had just put there.

"Don't, Augie," Darryl said. "Please!"

Augie pulled the bag up.

There was a rip in it.

As Augie lifted the bag, the rip got bigger.

The garbage was falling on the ground.

Augie stood back.

He stared at it.

There on the ground was a pulley, some rope, the clothespins.

"The parts from the automatic bed-maker," Augie said. "It's all there except for two aluminum rods. And you're throwing it all out?"

Darryl didn't say a word.

He didn't move either.

He just stared at Augie.

"I spent a week making you my best invention and you're throwing it out?" Augie asked.

"I told you not to butt in, Augie," Darryl said. "It wasn't like I was trying to let you know what I was doing with your invention!"

"I was just trying to help cheer you up after your mom got sick," Augie said. "So you'd feel better when you got home. And you toss it out with the garbage."

"I got a reason, Augie," Darryl said. "Only I just can't explain it to you. Not now."

60

"You and your stupid secrets," Augie sighed.

"They're not stupid," Darryl said. "I'll tell you as soon as I can."

"Forget it, Darryl," Augie said. "You're not my friend anymore."

"But Augie . . . ," Darryl cried.

"You don't treat friends the way you just treated me," Augie interrupted.

He started back to his house.

He could hear Darryl rolling over another garbage can.

He refused to look back.

He wasn't going to give Darryl that kind of satisfaction.

Not to an ex-friend, he wasn't.

Chapter Eight

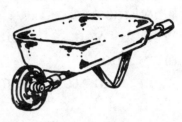

"You want to tell me what's up?"

His mom had asked him six times now and he still wasn't about to tell her.

Mr. Grimbly across the street had asked too.

Even Felicity had asked him why he was moping around lately.

But he couldn't explain it to anyone.

It just hurt too much to talk about what Darryl did to him.

Besides, how could Augie explain it when he didn't really understand it.

Now Rooney was asking him.

They were on their way to the pool in the park.

"Something's going on," Rooney said. "And Tara and I don't like it one bit. What's the secret, Augie?"

"I don't know any secret," Augie said.

The kids arrived at the hot dog stand.

"I'll buy you a hot dog if you tell me," Rooney said.

"You trying to bribe me?"

"You bet I am," Rooney said. "*Two* hot dogs, but you got to tell me *everything.*"

"I don't have any secrets, Rooney," Augie said.

"It's not about *your* secrets," Rooney said. "It's about what Darryl's doing these days. Tara and I can't figure it out. We hoped you'd know."

"I'm not talking to Darryl anymore," Augie said. "I don't want to talk *about* him either."

"Gee, what happened?" Rooney asked. "Wouldn't he tell you about it either?"

"Tell me about *what,* Rooney?" Augie asked.

"Operation Silver Secret?" Rooney said.

"What in the heck is Operation Silver Secret?"

"Well, it started because of all the silver foil," Rooney explained.

"Oh, that's no secret," Augie said. "Darryl's a silver foil freak. He's always collecting it."

"But where does he take it?" Rooney asked.

"He takes it somewhere?" Augie asked.

"Tara saw him take the wheelbarrow down the street three times, and each time the wheelbarrow was overflowing with silver foil," Rooney said. "When she asked him about it, he wouldn't say what he was doing with it."

"Gee," Augie said. "That *is* strange."

"And that's not the half of it either," Rooney said. "He was over at the McGuiness' yard sale and he wanted to buy the stainless steel, only he didn't have enough money. So he waited till the end, and when no one else bought it, he got Mrs. McGuiness to give it to him. Why would a kid want anyone's stainless steel?"

"Well, it's silver, isn't it," Augie said.

"But what's he doing with it?" Rooney asked. "And why did he ask if he could have Tara's mother's silverweed plant? And where was he going the other day with those silver poles?"

Augie stopped. "Silver poles?" he asked. "Real silver poles?"

"Aluminum poles," Rooney said. "But they're the color of silver, aren't they?"

"Aluminum poles?" Augie asked.

"About three feet long," Rooney said. "Couldn't be good for anything."

Suddenly Augie was excited. "They're from my automatic bed-maker, Rooney," he said. "They were the only part of it he didn't throw out!"

"Well, he was walking down Elm Street with them," Rooney said. "I tell you Darryl's up to something, and Tara and I are going to find out what it is. We don't like mysteries going on. Unless we're in on them."

"Well, if he's not going to tell you, you're never going to find out," Augie said.

"There are other ways to find out," Rooney said.

She was smiling.

The smile that always meant trouble.

"I don't want to know your other ways," Augie said suspiciously.

"We could stake out his house," Rooney said. "Keep it under a twenty-four-hour-a-day watch."

"Oh, that's just another one of your rotten tricks," Augie said.

"Is not," Rooney protested. "It's one of Tara's rotten tricks. She thought that one up. The part about trailing him is my idea."

"Like a detective?"

"Exactly," Rooney said. "We'd have to be really sharp about it. We don't want Darryl figuring out we're on to him. That's the easiest way to lose crooks."

"Darryl's not a crook," Augie said.

"How do you know for sure?" Rooney asked.

"No one looks less like a crook than Darryl," Augie said.

"It's the innocent-looking ones who always pull off the biggest crimes," Rooney assured him.

"Well, I don't want any part of it," Augie said. "It's not right to spy on someone, even Darryl."

"Consider it looking out for a friend," Rooney said.

"Forget it, Rooney," Augie said. "He's not my friend anymore."

"Forget it yourself," Rooney said.

They were almost to the pool in the park now.

"Look, Rooney," Augie said, "there's no way I'm going to be a spy. And I don't feel like swimming anymore, either."

"Suit yourself." Rooney waved to him and went off to the pool.

Augie wanted to steer clear of anything that could get him in trouble. And Rooney was always trouble!

But that evening, just before supper, he was in his room.

He looked at the place on the dresser where he had kept his silver dollar.

The special one that Uncle Bret had given to him on his last birthday. The one he had lent to Darryl.

Darryl had never returned it.

He looked out the window.

Darryl was pushing a wheelbarrow up his driveway.

Augie leaned out the window.

"Say, Darryl," Augie called. "You think you could return my silver dollar to me now?"

Darryl looked up.

"Not yet, Augie," he shouted back.

"How come?" Augie shouted.

"Can't tell you," Darryl said.

Darryl left the wheelbarrow next to the garage and went into his house.

Augie closed the window.

He went to the phone and dialed Rooney's number.

"Rooney," he said as soon as she came to the phone, "about Operation Silver Secret."

"What about it?" Rooney asked.

"I've changed my mind," Augie said. "Count me in!"

Chapter Nine

Every afternoon, just before supper, the three of them met over at Tara's house.

The first day it was Rooney's turn to report.

"Suspect left his house at precisely three o'clock," Rooney said as she checked her notes in a little spiral notebook.

"Was he carrying anything?" Augie asked.

"Another wheelbarrow of silver foil," Rooney reported. "I followed the suspect to the corner of Elm and Maple where I grilled him."

"You did *what?*" Tara asked.

"Well, I didn't exactly *grill* him," Rooney sighed. "I *asked* him where he was going.

To which the suspect replied, 'Leave me alone, Rooney.'"

"Sounds guilty to me!" Augie said.

"Something is definitely going on!" Tara exclaimed.

The second day it was Augie's turn.

He didn't need a notebook.

"Well, I saw him leave his house this afternoon," Augie said.

"At three o'clock?" Tara asked.

"At precisely three o'clock," Augie said. "And since questioning him didn't work for Rooney, I just followed him."

"Which direction did he go?" Rooney asked.

"Toward McKinley Street this time," Augie said.

"Was he carrying anything?" Rooney asked.

"Hubcaps," Augie said. "The ones his father's been keeping in his garage."

"*Silver* hubcaps?"

"Absolutely," Augie said. "When he got to the light, he turned around and saw me. I started running, but I couldn't catch up with him. Sorry about that."

"We'll just have to work on our strategy," Rooney said. "We're going to crack Operation Silver Secret if it's the last thing we do!"

The new plan meant another meeting.

It also meant a trip to the Quick Mart for whistles.

The day after, at precisely three o'clock, the kids were at their stations.

Rooney was at the traffic light, hiding behind the mailbox at the corner.

Tara waited at the other end of the block.

She was hiding in the doorway of her cousin's house.

Augie would wait on the other side of the block.

Those were the only three routes Darryl could take.

One of the kids was bound to see him.

The kid who saw him first was supposed to blow his whistle.

The other two would blow back.

Then they would come running.

Secretly, they would follow Darryl the rest of the way.

At five minutes after three, Augie was hiding behind Mr. Lomack's Ford Escort on the other side of the block.

He waited.

And waited.

He saw a kid coming around the side of the Lomacks' house.

He peered over the hood of the car.

It was Felicity.

And she was carrying a doll.

Forget it.

Augie looked at his watch again.

Eight minutes after three o'clock.

He waited some more.

He looked at his watch again.

"Oooooh! Oooooh! Oooooh!

It was a whistle.

It blew again.

It was coming from the other end of the block.

It was Tara!

Augie blew on his whistle.

He heard Rooney blowing too.

Then he started running.

He ran across the Lomacks' lawn.

Around their house and through their backyard.

He jumped the fence.

He ran around the Peetries' house.

When he came out on Maple Street, he saw Rooney.

She was running down the sidewalk.

Together they ran toward the park.

Tara was at the corner.

She was holding the whistle.

She blew it again.

She pointed to the park.

There was Darryl.

He was walking around the fountain.

He was carrying Tara's mother's silver-weed plant.

Augie and Tara and Rooney followed quietly.

Darryl was going by the rock garden.

They waited behind the locust trees.

He was going by the playground.

The kids hid behind the hot dog stand.

They ran after him until he got to the other side of the park.

He was waiting for the light.

When he crossed the street, they dashed behind him and hid behind a picket fence on the other side.

He walked down the street.

One block.

Then another.

He turned to the right.

"My gosh!" Augie whispered. "He's going to Mrs. Ames's!"

They peered around Mrs. Ames's house.

"He's going into her garage!" Tara sighed.

"Why would he do that?" Rooney asked.

The kids hid in the bushes.

They waited almost fifteen minutes.

Then they saw Mrs. Ames leave the garage.

Darryl was following.

They got in her car.

When the car had disappeared, Augie and Rooney and Tara stepped out from behind the fence.

"What are we supposed to do now?" Tara said.

"Check out the garage," Rooney said.

"What if it's locked?" Augie asked.

Augie stepped up to the door.

He pushed.

It wasn't locked.

"Even if it's open, we're still trespassing," Tara said. "Maybe we shouldn't."

But it was too late.

Rooney was already inside.

Tara and Augie followed her.

The garage wasn't a garage anymore.

It was a studio.

The big doors had been replaced by windows.

The cement floor was wood now.

The roof was mostly a skylight.

But the room was empty.

Almost.

At the far end was something the likes of which Augie had never seen before.

It was very, very big.

It was also very, very silver.

The sun coming through the skylight made it gleam.

"It's so beautiful," Rooney gasped.

"It's *like* a painting," Tara said.

"Only it's not paint," Augie whispered. "It's got all sorts of things in it."

"There's all the stainless steel stuck all over!" Tara exclaimed.

"And all the aluminum foil," Rooney said.

Augie stepped closer.

With every step he could see another silver thing he hadn't seen before.

The aluminum poles from the automatic bed-maker. The hubcaps. The sprigs from Tara's mother's silverweed plant.

Something at the very center of it gleamed in the sunlight.

Augie stepped closer.

It wasn't until he could almost reach out and touch it that he knew for sure the center piece was the silver dollar.

Chapter Ten

The kids couldn't stop staring at the silver thing with all the silver things in it.

They walked closer to it.

They touched parts of it.

They were looking at it so hard that they didn't hear the car in the driveway.

They didn't hear the car door slam.

They didn't hear Mrs. Ames entering the studio.

"It's beautiful, isn't it?"

Augie turned suddenly.

Right away, he knew they shouldn't have come into the studio without permission.

"We didn't mean to come in," Augie stammered.

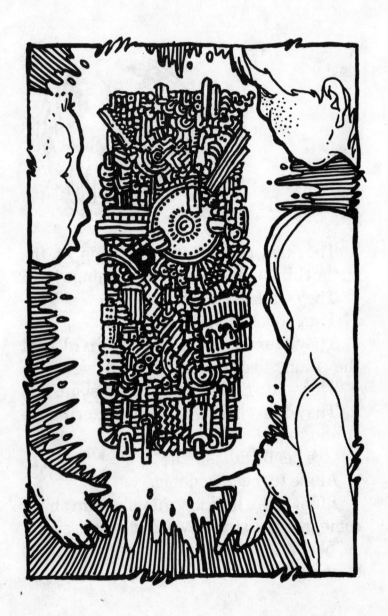

"It's just that we were following Darryl," Rooney said.

"We've been worried," Tara added.

"Well, next time, do ask first," Mrs. Ames said. "But this time it's okay. I've wanted you all to see it when it was done."

"It's sort of weird, but it's beautiful too," Augie said.

"It's kind of like art," Tara said.

"It *is* art," Mrs. Ames said. "It's very beautiful art too."

"It's got all the silver stuff Darryl's been collecting," Augie said.

"He was collecting them for you, Mrs. Ames, so you could put them all together," Tara said.

"Look at the right-hand bottom," Mrs. Ames said.

Augie looked in the corner.

"It says Darryl Lenski," Augie said. "What's Darryl's name doing there at the bottom of the thing, Mrs. Ames?"

"Oh, it's what we call a collage," Mrs. Ames said. "And I didn't have a thing to do with it."

"But you're an artist," Rooney said.

"It's all Darryl's work."

"Darryl?" Rooney asked. "All by himself?"

"He's an artist?" Tara asked.

"He's a very talented artist," Mrs. Ames said. "He's been working on that collage ever since he got back from his aunt's."

"Is this where he comes every afternoon at three?" Augie asked.

"Exactly," Mrs. Ames said. "For two or three hours every afternoon. He's really remarkable."

"But he wouldn't tell us," Augie said. "Why the big secret?"

"Maybe he couldn't tell you," Mrs. Ames said.

"I'm supposed to be his best friend," Augie said. "That means he's supposed to tell me everything."

"Augie, things are different now for Darryl," Mrs. Ames said.

"What do you mean different?" Augie asked.

"On account of his mother, you mean?" Tara asked.

"You explained all that," Augie said. "About how addiction's a disease and it doesn't mean Mrs. Lenski's a bad person. But Mrs. Lenski's getting help. That's all over. It doesn't have anything to do with Darryl and me."

"When someone in a family is ill, particularly someone with an addiction problem, it changes things for all the other people in a family," Mrs. Ames said. "The sick person is getting all the attention, even though they don't really mean to. Everyone else gets less attention."

"That's why Darryl needs friends more than ever," Augie said. "That's why I asked him to work with me on my inventions."

"I invited him to my birthday party and he didn't come," Tara added.

"I wanted him to make water bombs with me," Rooney said.

"But those are all things *you* wanted to do, kids," Mrs. Ames said. "When he's with one of you, he feels like a little kid, like someone's helper. Whatever he's doing with you, it's more about you than it is about Darryl."

"But he always went along," Augie sighed.

"Everyone changes," Mrs. Ames said. "Darryl needs something all his own now. Something where he's the leader. And thank heavens he took to the artwork. I'm entering his collage in an art show next week, and I wouldn't be at all surprised if he walks off with a ribbon, Augie."

Augie heard the door slam.

He turned.

Darryl was standing behind him.

"Gee, Darryl," Tara said. "We didn't know you were an artist!"

"It's just a start," Darryl said.

"But it's wonderful," Rooney said. "Mrs. Ames says she's entering it in a contest too."

"I'm sorry I didn't tell you about it," Darryl said. "All of you, but you especially, Augie. I know you're mad at me."

"You should have told me what you were up to," Augie said.

"I was afraid, Augie," Darryl admitted.

"You can't be afraid of me," Augie said. "I'm your friend."

"I was afraid you'd want to do it too," Darryl said. "Heck, Augie, I was just afraid you'd do it better than I did."

"You got no reason to be afraid," Augie said.

"Remember a couple years ago when I wanted to be an inventor?" Darryl asked. "You wanted to help at first. But right away you got to be boss and I got to be your assistant."

Augie was silent. He'd forgotten all about it.

Darryl went to the collage. He pulled the silver dollar from the center of it and handed it to Augie.

"Thanks," Augie said.

He put the silver dollar in his pocket.

"I'm sorry it's different for you now, Darryl," he said.

He walked to the door.

But he didn't open it.

He turned around and walked to the collage.

He reached into his pocket for the silver dollar and stuck it in the center of Darryl's silver secret.

"But it's your Uncle Bret's," Darryl said. "It's your special silver dollar."

"It looks a lot better in your collage than on my dresser," Augie said. "I want it to stay right where it is. It belongs in the center of your collage."

"Thank you, Augie," Darryl said.

"I'm sorry I tried to turn you into my little assistant," Augie said.

"You know, just because I'm an artist now, doesn't mean I don't want to be friends," Darryl said.

"I'd rather have a friend than a little helper," Augie said.

Darryl was smiling.

So was Augie.

It didn't feel like he'd lost an old friend after all.

It was more like getting a brand new one.